Unusual Day

Sandi Toksvig

Illustrated by

Georgien Overwater

CORGI PUPS

To Jesse, Meg and Bear

UNUSUAL DAY
A CORGI PUPS BOOK : 0 552 545392

First publication in Great Britain

PRINTING HISTORY
Corgi Pups edition published 1997
10 9

Set in Bembo Schoolbook

Corgi Pups Books are published by Transworld Publishers,
61-63 Uxbridge Road, London W5 5SA,
a division of The Random House Group Ltd,
in Australia by Random House Australia (Pty) Ltd,
20 Alfred Street, Milsons Point, Sydney, NSW 2061, Australia,
in New Zealand by Random House New Zealand Ltd,
18 Poland Road, Glenfield, Auckland 10, New Zealand
and in South Africa by Random House (Pty) Ltd,
Endulini, 5a Jubilee Road, Parktown 2193, South Africa.

Made and printed in Great Britain by
Mackays of Chatham plc, Chatham, Kent

Contents

Series Reading Consultant: Prue Goodwin,
Reading and Language Information Centre,
University of Reading

Chapter One

Blue Class were having an
'Unusual Day'. Well, there was
nothing unusual about the day
itself. Everyone had been to
assembly as usual, everyone had
done quiet reading as usual and

everyone had drunk their juice in
break as usual. It was after lunch
that the unusual part was to
happen.

All the children had been asked
to bring in something 'unusual'
to talk about. The idea had
started with Blue Class having a
'Blue Day' where everyone had
to bring in something blue.

Then they had had a 'Nature Day' where everyone had to bring something from the garden, followed by 'Pet Day'. 'Pet Day' had not been entirely successful. All the dogs, cats and hamsters had behaved very well, but

Kristian's snake had gone
missing. The classroom had been
turned upside down looking for
Barry the Boa.

The snake finally turned up ten
minutes before the bell in the
Rainy Day Box. Mrs Robinson,
who played piano on Tuesdays,
had found him. It was a shame
Barry had given her such a fright,

but everyone had had such fun playing hospital while they waited for her to come round. Blue Class's teacher, Miss Johnson, who has very red hair and is in charge, says there won't be music on Tuesdays this term.

Today, however, was 'Unusual Day'. Miss Johnson had told the children they could bring in anything that was really different. Joey had brought a doll from Russia called a 'Babushka'.

It was made of brightly painted wood and had lots of other dolls inside it. Kristian had brought a nappy from his baby sister. She had worn it all night and it was still dry. His mother had said it was 'most unusual'. Esme, who had been a big hit on 'Nature

Day' with her slug collection, had found a four-leafed clover.

As they arrived, everyone had put their unusual things on the big table so that Miss Johnson

could label them. Jessica Grace
was late.

"Hello Jessica," said Miss
Johnson, putting someone's three-
legged *My Little Pony* at the back
of the table. "Have you brought
something unusual today?"

"Yes," said Jessica. "She's
outside."

"She?" asked Miss Johnson.
Jessica nodded. "I've brought
my granny."

Chapter Two

"Your granny?" Miss Johnson
looked down at Jessica. "I don't
think you've understood, Jessica.
Today is 'Unusual Day'. You
were supposed to bring

something different. Something
unusual. 'Family Day' isn't until
next week. You can bring Granny
on 'Family Day'."

Just then Jessica's granny came
into the room. Jessica's granny

looked quite like a granny. She
had grey hair like a granny and
lines on her face like a granny.
She did have a tracksuit and
trainers on, but other than that
Miss Johnson really didn't think
she looked unusual at all.

Anyway, all the unusual things
were supposed to go on the big
table and have a label put on
them. It was a bit difficult
to put a granny in amongst
the snails with painted shells,

a sand painting from Tunisia and a barometer shaped like a pixie from Bracklesham Bay.

"I'm awfully sorry," Miss
Johnson said to Jessica's granny.
"You're welcome to stay, but I'm
afraid Jessica hasn't quite
understood about 'Unusual Day'.
She was supposed to bring
something out of the ordinary.
Something the others might not
see every day."

Jessica's granny said she understood and would come back next week. She kissed Jessica and left.

That afternoon all the other children stood up one by one and explained their unusual things. Jessica wasn't paying attention. She was cross. Even Reuben's

Australian hat and Katie's doll
which could yodel the Austrian
National Anthem didn't interest
her. Jessica knew her granny
would have been the most unusual
of all.

Jessica had
met other
grannies.
They cooked
and sewed
and slept
through the
news. Hers
built walls,
retiled the
roof and spent
one summer
digging her
own
swimming
pool. Other
grannies
knitted for a
hobby.

Jessica's went windsurfing. Not
all the time. When there was no
wind she went roller-skating.

Jessica did perk up a bit at
Matthew's turn. He'd brought in
his sister's doll which someone

had fed real porridge. He was just
showing everyone that it now had
a black tummy under its dress
when Kristian noticed the smoke.

"I think there's a fire," said
Kristian loudly.

"Kristian," said Miss Johnson,
"please, wait your turn. Matthew
hasn't finished with his doll yet."

"Well, if there isn't a fire, then
someone's having a barbecue
in the playground."

Kristian was bored with
unusual things and thought even
the most ordinary of fires would
be much more exciting.

"Shall I have a look?" said
Jessica.

"Fire, fire!" Reuben and some of the other boys started chanting while Esme began beating time on her desk with a Russian doll.

"But it's my turn to speak!" bawled Phoebe, who was next after Matthew. "I've got a sand crab with a face like *Paddington Bear*." And she burst into tears.

The morning was not going as well as Miss Johnson had hoped. "Boys! Esme! Phoebe, you're too old for this kind of thing."

Just then Peter the caretaker appeared in the doorway.

"Miss Johnson, Blue Class," he said, "I don't want you to be alarmed. I'm afraid the house next door is on fire. The children are quite safe in here. I've called the fire brigade."

Down the road the children
could hear sirens coming closer.
Kristian and Jessica could not sit
for another moment. They
rushed to the window. Across the
playground they could see smoke
pouring out of the large Victorian

house next to the school. Soon
all the children were gathered
round the windows to see the fire
engines arrive.

"Here comes one!" shouted
Reuben as a giant red truck
pulled up outside.

"And another!" cried Esme.

Soon three enormous fire
engines filled the car park and
firemen in blue uniforms and
hard yellow hats swarmed
outside the building. Hose-pipes
and ladders appeared from
everywhere.

"Look!" said Jessica. "It's Mrs
Heathrington!"

Chapter Three

Everyone in Blue Class knew Mrs
Heathrington. She waved to
them every morning and once a
week brought in biscuits for them
all. She was very good at baking
and although she was very old,

she knew a surprising amount
about the records of Michael
Jackson.

In the very top window of the
smoking building the children
could just see the old lady. She

was calling down to the people below. Smoke gushed all round her and soon it was difficult to see her properly.

The firemen quickly winched their ladder round to the window and one of them began to climb. For a short moment at the top of the ladder, the fireman disappeared altogether in the smoke. The children cheered as

he reappeared carrying Mrs
Heathrington on his shoulder.

"My word," said Miss Johnson,
still trying to get Phoebe to stop
crying.

Miss Johnson opened the class door out into the playground and waved to the firemen. "You can bring Mrs Heathrington in here if you like."

The children stood back as
two firemen brought the old
lady into the classroom. Mrs
Heathrington had soot on her
face and looked very tired.
Jessica got her a chair. Kristian

offered her the rest of his
blackcurrant drink but she didn't
seem interested.

"My Bunsie, my Bunsie," Mrs
Heathrington whispered over and
over.

"You're all right," said Miss

Johnson soothingly. "You're all
right, Mrs Heathrington."

"My Bunsie, my Bunsie," the
old woman kept repeating.

Miss Johnson patted her hand
and then took Phoebe off to
change her pants.

"Bunsie's her rabbit," said
Jessica knowledgeably. "Her
rabbit must still be in the house!"

"The rabbit, the rabbit!" the
whole of Blue Class began
shouting across to the firemen.
"Mrs Heathrington's rabbit is still
inside."

Through the haze, the children could see a fireman in his yellow helmet climbing back up the long ladder. The bright hat disappeared through the smoke and into the top window.

The children fell silent as they watched.

"Do you think Bunsie will be OK?" whispered Kristian.

"Absolutely," said Jessica, although she didn't feel sure.

They had to wait a long time. Longer than it took Jessica's

Uncle Charlie to explain why sums are so simple. At last the fireman reappeared in the window.

"Where's the rabbit?" said Esme.

"He hasn't got the rabbit," said Katie.

"My Bunsie, my Bunsie," said Mrs Heathrington.

No-one said a word. The
fireman climbed slowly down the
long ladder. At the bottom, he
turned and reached inside his
jacket. Suddenly a great cheer
went up from the class.

"It's in his jacket!" shouted
Kristian. "He's got it in his
jacket."

From inside his heavy blue coat,
the fireman pulled out the
coughing rabbit. He held the
bewildered bunny up for the
children to see and they began

dancing and singing around Mrs
Heathrington.

"Bunsie's safe, Bunsie's safe!"

Chapter Four

"I'd better see if we can get the firemen some tea," said Miss Johnson coming back in with Phoebe.

Soon the fire was out and just a little smoke lingered in the air.

The firemen began winding up
their hoses and Miss Johnson
called them in to have tea in the
hall. Their great boots made
muddy tracks across the wooden
floor but even Miss Walton, the
headmistress, didn't seem to mind.

"Miss Johnson, Granny wants a word," said Jessica to Miss Johnson who was handing out custard creams.

"Not just now, Jessica," said Miss Johnson. "I told you, Granny can come on 'Family Day'."

"But she wants to know if Blue Class can look after Bunsie while Mrs Heathrington stays with her sister."

Miss Johnson was confused.

Jessica led her over to the fireman
who had rescued Bunsie. Miss
Johnson looked carefully at the
uniformed officer. The fireman
took off his hat. Except he wasn't
a 'he' at all. Standing in front of

Miss Johnson, in a dirty fireman's uniform and with a smudged face, was Jessica's granny.

"You're a ... I mean you ... " Miss Johnson could hardly speak. "You went up the ladder ... and ... Mrs Heathrington ... your shoulder ... "

Miss Johnson had to sit down. It was Jessica's granny who had rescued Mrs Heathrington and Jessica's granny who had gone back for the rabbit. Jessica's granny was the fireman.

"I'm sorry Jessica," said Miss Johnson. "I see why you wanted your granny here on 'Unusual Day'. It really is most unusual to have a granny who is a fireman."

"Oh, that isn't why I brought her," said Jessica who had never thought of Granny's job as different. "I think Granny's

unusual because she can spin
plates. Mum says she just wishes
Granny wouldn't do it with food
still on them!"

THE END